TEMPTING SHADOW

Margo Davis

Copyright © 2024 Margo Davis

All rights reserved

The characters and events portrayed in this book are fictitious. Any similarity to real persons, living or dead, is coincidental and not intended by the author.

No part of this book may be reproduced, or stored in a retrieval system, or transmitted in any form or by any means, electronic, mechanical, photocopying, recording, or otherwise, without express written permission of the publisher.

Cover design by: Margo Davis

Author's Note

Tempting Shadow is a quick and easy story, with the intention of being a light read. I didn't aim for deep, complex storytelling. Instead, it is a simple but extremely spicy novelette.
Therefore, I ask you to not take this book too seriously. It features a monster, after all, and we all know those aren't real.
And yes, for those who say that this is pure monster corn...that's exactly what it is.
Also, the monster in this book does not speak our language well. This means that his sentences are worded strangely at times.

Enjoy!

CHAPTER 1

PENELOPE

Ever since I was a child, I had been fascinated by the stories of the creatures who lived in the Land of Everything. People called it that because there was nothing the human mind could imagine that didn't live there.

I had been reading my grandmother's old books again for the past six months. The ones she used to keep hidden in her attic, but always went to get whenever I begged for her to read one to me. They weren't really children's books, and maybe my grandma should've been more strict because the first couple of times she read those stories to me, I had nightmares.

Still, I ended up growing up with those stories, and the older I got, the more I understood the significance of the connection the Land of Everything had with the real world.

Many different books had been written about the creatures over the past couple of decades, and there would still be many to come, but the one that stuck with me the most was the story about the shadow creature who lived in the caves in the Land of

Everything.

To this day, I couldn't stop thinking about *him*.

That one specific shadow creature from that one specific book.

Today I had been thinking about it again, and after getting it off my bookshelf, I admired the cover, nervous but excited to dive into it again.

In the beginning, it was hard to understand what was real and what wasn't. The authors of these books marked them as fictional, but most people knew that the creatures existed, and that some people were stupid enough to go look for them. There were also different communities of shifters and hybrids, which were the undeniable proof that at least some of the stories were true.

The book I was holding in my hands seemed to have been written about real events that took place too.

At least to me they were real. I believed most of the stories, but there were some absurd ones that sounded too crazy to be true.

This book was about a woman who went to the Land of Everything, hopeful to get help from the shadow creature. It was a hard winter for her, and she had no food for her family. She was willing to offer *her* shadow to him, in return for meat he would hunt.

When I was little, I didn't understand what she was really giving him. Clearly, no human could give their shadow to someone else. But as I got older, I realized that the shadow was just a metaphor the author used to make the book more…kid-friendly.

In fact, the woman offered her body to the creature.

The story ended abruptly after the woman mated with the shadow creature, leaving me wondering what happened to them, and where they were now.

Lying back on my bed, I began to study the sketch of the creature in the book. I had done that many times before, just admiring it.

It was supposed to be a sixteen-foot-tall, demon-like figure with two large horns and a long tail. It was magnificent on paper and I wondered if it would be just as impressive if I ever saw it with my own eyes.

A while ago, I began to feel a strong pull toward the creature, as if it was calling out to me. It was extremely tempting to go out there and find it, and the strange feeling in my lower stomach made me want to give in and stop resisting.

"It's too dangerous," I whispered as I grazed the sketch of the creature with my fingertips. "But it might be worth it."

I sat up again, with the book still in my hands, and the creature's eyes staring right back into my soul. It was foolish of me to believe that there was a connection between us, but I had never had an adventurous idea like this, and somehow, I felt the urge to prove to myself that something in my life would change if I only went to look for him.

I carefully tore the sketch out of the book and folded the paper in half, placing it on my nightstand.

It was then that I decided that tomorrow, I would set out to find him. He who had been reappearing in my dreams for months, and who gave me the most intense feelings I had ever felt.

***

It was the next morning, and the first thing I did was pack everything I needed for my trip. Two bottles of water and a loaf of bread landed in my backpack, as well as two blankets and a raincoat.

After eating breakfast and drinking enough water, I ventured out to the forest. The air was still cool, and I wished I had thought of bringing gloves to keep my hands warm.

I had my blonde hair tied back into a ponytail, and with my ears exposed to the coldness, I wished I had brought a beanie as well. I had high hopes that the sun would be warming me up soon, but in the forest, and with the trees surrounding me, there was little way for the sun to shine through.

"Just keep on walking," I told myself to keep warm.

The forest separated the human realm from the Land of Everything, and it didn't take me long before I made it to the river that ran through the valley of the Ash Mountains.

The caves in which the shadow creatures lived were supposed to be on the other side of those mountains, and while it was said that no human had ever set foot inside, I couldn't help but believe that some already had.

How else were those books written with such conviction about how those caves looked like?

Either way, I was going into one.

I needed to look for that creature that had been messing with my mind for so long.

With each step I took, the strange feeling in my belly became more intense. It wasn't painful, but it wasn't necessarily pleasant either, and I started to believe that me getting closer to the cave had something to do with it.

But even after walking all day, I wasn't close to it at all. I stopped a couple of times along the way, making sure I was going the right direction, and occasionally drinking and eating the things I brought with me. I had no idea how long this trip would've become, and I made sure to put aside a few things so I wouldn't run out on my way back home.

When the darkness slowly rolled in, I made the decision to stop. I had been walking for hours, and not only my feet hurt. A recurring stomach cramp made me want to lie down.

I found a big tree I could get comfortable under, and while it didn't seem like the safest thing to do in the middle of this forest, there was no better place to take a break.

It took a while for my body to relax, but even after the stomach cramps had gotten less thanks to me lying down, I couldn't fall asleep. My body and mind felt strange, and the sudden cold sweat running down my neck worried me. I felt uncomfortable and hazy, and the animalistic noises and howls echoing through the dense forest weren't exactly helping me find sleep either.

The tension inside of me built rapidly, only to find no release. It was exhausting, but I had to keep moving. I needed to find help, and instead of going back home where I knew I'd be safe, I was pulled further into the forest.

Closer to the caves, and closer to the shadow creature.

CHAPTER 2

PENELOPE

Even with the moonlight shining through the top of the trees, it wasn't bright enough for me to see where I was going. Luckily, I had brought a flashlight with me, and I used it to guide me through the darkness.

I kept on walking, trying to be aware of my surroundings at all times. With this vision-blurring headache though, it wasn't so easy. My feet kept on carrying me for a while longer, but every once in a while, the stomach cramps got so bad that I had to stop and crouch down until the pain eased.

Even with all this pain, it didn't occur to me to mind even once that what I was doing was extremely stupid.

"I'm out of my goddamn mind," I murmured with my face pressed against my knees before standing back up again. I couldn't shake the idea of this going horribly wrong, but that strong urge pulling me toward those creatures was simply too intense.

I kept walking until I noticed that the trees had become less, and the moon was fully visible up in the night sky. I lowered my flashlight as I looked up at the moon to admire it.

It might've been the headache causing me to imagine things, but the moon looked so much closer and bigger here than it did back home. My eyes started itching the longer I stared up at the moon. Lowering my head again, I closed my eyes and took a deep breath.

The pain was back again, only much stronger this time.

"Ouch…" I cried out, bending over with my arms crossed over my belly. "Make it stop."

I heard a deep growl close by, and when I looked up, there was an opening to a cave that I hadn't noticed.

No way this is real, I thought. *That wasn't there before.*

Another cramp hit me, and I fell to my knees, unable to hold myself up any longer. "God…please," I whispered, gasping for air.

I needed anyone, *anything*, to help me. This pain was unbearable.

Another growl echoed from the cave, and I started to crawl toward it. I was hopeful–and fairly delusional–to get help from whoever, no, *whatever* was in there. My eyes were watery, and when the darkness of the cave slowly swallowed me, there was nothing else to do then let it take me.

"Please help," I whispered, my voice sounding as weak as my body felt.

"Stupid human." An animalistic voice came from the inside, and it sent shivers down my spine.

With my body tense and fear creeping up on me, I lifted my head to get a closer look. It was too dark to see, and when the first couple of cramps hit, I had dropped my flashlight.

I patted down the ground around me, trying to find it, but with my mind spinning and my body not working properly, I couldn't get to it.

Tears rolled down my face just as another cramp made my stomach twist, and I whimpered, unable to move. "Please," I begged again.

At that point, I had no idea what I was begging for. I needed help, but I wasn't sure anymore that I wanted it from that thing with the insanely deep voice.

Heavy footsteps made the ground shake as they came closer. I tried my hardest to see what was coming toward me, and through my blurred vision, I could see a giant, dark figure appear.

I tilted my head, needing to see all of it, and a pair of golden, glowing eyes stared down into mine. My breath caught in my throat, unwillingly making me hold my breath as I finally understood whose cave I had invaded.

I found him.

But why did his presence physically hurt?

I couldn't stop staring at him, and the intensity of him simply standing there in the darkness was too much for me to handle. I wanted to get back on my feet, but my knees were weak.

I felt like running.

Even though I had found who I was looking for, I

wanted to run back home.

The pain was simply too much.

It was exhausting.

"It is too late now." His words sounded carefully chosen, and though his pronunciation was good, it seemed as if he hadn't been talking for too long.

He took another step toward me, and thanks to the moonlight, I could now see his full being. His two curved horns were just like in the drawing, but his head was much bigger.

Just like his body.

I underestimated how tall sixteen feet were.

Then again, I lived in a world where most people barely grew up to be six feet tall. Giants only existed here. In this realm. In the Land of Everything.

"I don't understand," I whispered. "This pain…"

"It is your fate. It was sealed the moment you crossed the river," he explained, sounding determined in his words. "You need me the same way I need you, human."

I tried to understand what he meant, but my mind was still fogged up. I kept looking up at him, and the closer he got, the stranger the pain became. It somehow eased but got worse at the same time, and my legs felt dumb, as if I had just ran a marathon.

To be fair, I did walk for hours without getting any sleep.

"I don't understand," I said quietly. "I don't know why I'm feeling this way."

He reached out his large hand, and with one big

claw he brushed aside a strand of my hair that had fallen out of my ponytail. I shivered, unable to move. The short fur of his hand caressed my cheek, and that one simple touch made me whimper.

He growled again, but this time it didn't sound scary. It sounded almost like a purr. "We are meant to be. Our souls have been bound. Though…" he paused and looked me up and down with his glowing eyes as his nose curled up in disgust. "I do not know why I was given a weak human female."

"Excuse you?"

He stood there as if he hadn't just insulted me, and while I wanted to get angry, I couldn't. The pain was back, and I curled into a ball, with my arms wrapped around my legs.

I couldn't comprehend what was happening, but there was an undeniable pull between us. I didn't want to believe what he was saying. I knew about fated mates, though those were rare. Especially between two breeds that were so different.

He wasn't just a simple shadow creature. He was a giant. He was way too large to have a fated mate like me. A human. A tiny one at that.

"We aren't compatible," I croaked out, lifting my head again to look at him. I managed to get back on my knees, but I kept my arms around my stomach to try and ease this ever-growing pain.

If he was made for me, why on earth would it hurt so terribly being near him? Wasn't he supposed to help? To make me feel good?

And while having those thoughts, I remembered

something I read a while ago.

My eyes widened, and I stared at him, unable to speak.

I needed to be released from this pain, and the only one who could do it was my fated mate. But there was no way he would…fit.

"We are compatible," he assured me, looking rather confused himself as he probably was still thinking about how weak of a woman I was. *Asshole*.

"Maybe it's a mistake," I argued.

"Fate does not make mistakes," he murmured as he crouched down in front of me. With his face closer to mine, I could finally see him well enough to admire his magnificence.

His face looked like it was carved out of stone, and his jaw was strong and defined. His lips were a light shade of violet, contrasting his golden eyes. His nose was wide, and his big nostrils flared as he started sniffing me.

"You smell delicious."

Gee…thanks?

I swallowed hard, unable to take my eyes off him. There was no way this would work. Hell, I could fit in the palm of his hand, and that's the only thing that would *fit*.

How would he be able to make this pain go away, if he would literally be able to tear me apart?

I closed my eyes tightly and shook my head to stop overthinking. I couldn't keep imagining things that would probably never happen. They were silly thoughts anyway.

As I opened my eyes again, I watched as he reached out his hand, and I froze as I realized what he was up to. He wrapped his large fingers around me, picking me off the floor as if I was a feather. To be fair, I was tiny. Five feet were nothing. At least in my family it wasn't, but I clearly was the exception.

I didn't argue. I couldn't, because I didn't have the strength to.

The pain was too much, and the way he was staring at me distracted me. He was looking at me as if he was trying to figure out what he wanted to do with me next.

"You are in pain but we can not mate. You must recover. Sleep, eat, drink."

I furrowed my brows. "Mate?"

He looked at me like I was stupid. "Yes. You are in pain because we have to mate. But we can not mate because you are weak."

Although it sounded like he was insulting me, he didn't look too happy with the state I was in.

I hadn't slept in a while, and all the walking was exhausting. But where would I sleep? A cave didn't sound very comfortable.

"If you want me to recover and sleep, I will need a bed. A warm and soft one," I told him. I was holding on to his thumb which was curled around the front of my body, and I watched him as intently as he was watching me.

"You sleep on me."

I raised a brow. "What?"

"You sleep on me. Here," he said, patting his chest

with his other hand.

"You want me to sleep on you?"

"Yes. We do not have beds. The female sleeps on the male."

I frowned. "Always?"

"Yes." He looked frustrated with me for asking so many questions. "You sleep on me," he repeated, looking determined.

Making him angry was the last thing I wanted. I was too tired to argue anyway, and while it sounded like the most irrational thing ever, I decided to simply agree with him. I needed sleep, and since he was my fated mate…there was no way he would hurt me while I slept.

"Okay. I will try to sleep on your chest."

It sounded like a stupid thing to do, but his fur was soft and cozy, and he could keep me warm. It was better than sleeping on the cold floor, and in a way, I trusted this strange creature.

"We walk you home. My home."

He moved his hand and made me lay against the crook of his arm. At this point, I wasn't asking any more questions. I made myself comfortable, and the more I relaxed, the more I noticed the intense pain vanish. Being close to him helped to ease the cramps, but to make them fully disappear, I would have to let him mate with me.

"Isn't this your home?" I asked, looking around the cave we were in.

"No. I live deeper."

I wondered when and where he started to

speak my language. It wasn't perfect, but I could understand him well enough, even if he didn't elaborate on his words much.

"How deep into this cave do you live?" I asked.

"Deep."

I rolled my eyes at his response, muttering under my breath how helpful that answer was.

"Do not roll your eyes." He looked down at me with a stern expression. "It is not nice."

Right.

I forgot that even in this world, I had to be polite and have manners. Because this sixteen-feet-tall shadow creature had them too, clearly.

"How did you know I would be here?"

"I felt it."

"Did you feel pain too?" I wondered, looking up at him.

His glowing eyes met mine as he started walking toward the darkness. He looked amused. "Yes. But I can handle pain. I am not weak like you."

"Hey!" I slapped his chest but it felt like punching a pillow. "I'm not weak! Usually…"

He grunted and shook his head as his arm nudged me tighter against his chest. "Sleep. It will take a while to reach the other side of the mountain."

The darkness overcame us, and the only thing I saw were his eyes. I wanted to ask if he was even able to see, but I figured he could. He was a shadow creature after all, and in the books I read about his kind, it said that they mostly lived in darkness.

I closed my eyes as a wave of comfort washed

over me, and I turned more toward him to curl up against his warmth. In a matter of seconds I was asleep, and I found myself in the deepest sleep I've had in a while.

CHAPTER 3

PENELOPE

I woke up with a hole in my stomach, and with rays of sunlight shining onto my face. Opening my eyes, I squinted against the light and moved my hand to cover my face.

Without having to look around, I knew exactly where I was. Well, I didn't see where he had taken me yet, but I was still lying on him. Instead of the crook of his arm I had fallen asleep in, I was now on his chest, feeling it rising and falling as he breathed.

His big hand was covering me, with his thumb resting on my neck, and his *little* finger grazing my lower back. His hand was like a warm blanket, and although I had no idea where I was exactly, I felt protected.

The pain in my belly was still there, but it had turned into a more bearable kind of ache. I didn't want to move, but I wanted to see where he had taken me.

I opened my eyes and lifted my head to look around, but he immediately pushed me back down, holding me in place.

"You need to rest," he growled, his chest

vibrating.

I put my head back down, frowning at his demand. "I think I've slept enough," I argued.

"No." He caressed my back with one of his fingertips, running it up and down the length of my spine. "It was not enough. Relax."

I took a deep breath and decided to obey him.

I stayed on top of him for a while longer, and stared straight ahead at the entrance which let in enough sunlight. That was the only place the sun was shining into though, because from above, there was more light coming in.

I still had to figure out where exactly he had taken me, and what this home of his looked like. But there was still time for that. I wasn't in a rush, and leaving hadn't crossed my mind yet.

Running my hand through his fur, I waited for more time to pass until he would let me get up and explore. The fact that I was lying on a shadow creature's chest was insane. I was still amazed by the way he looked, and by his incredible size. I used to study the sketch of him, never imagining him actually looking just like in the drawing.

But whoever had drawn that sketch made it fairly accurate.

Thanks to the drawing, he had also appeared in my dreams many times before, and even there, he looked just like he did in real life.

The only thing that hadn't been accurate were his eyes.

More time had passed, and I turned my head to

look up at him. I've had enough of lying down, and so I pushed myself up, hoping he would finally let me get off him.

His hand moved away, and as he sat up, I slid down his body until my feet hit the ground. I took a couple of steps away from him to get a better look, and his eyes followed me closely. They looked even more golden because of the sunlight, and they gave me a sense of warmth as I stared into them.

"How are you feeling, human?" he asked.

I thought about his questions for a while, unsure of how to answer.

How *did* I feel?

Overwhelmed?

Confused?

Yes, those were the right words.

"I'm feeling many things," I told him.

I felt the connection between us, but it was still strange to think that he was my fated mate. There was an invisible string between us. Something humans usually didn't have since there was no magic in our world.

He slowly nodded and lifted a hand, carefully brushing a strand of my hair out of my face. My ponytail was loose, and I desperately needed to fix it.

I found myself leaning into his touch, but I quickly moved back, torn between this insane pull toward him, and the unknown that still lingered around me.

Tilting my head to the side, I studied him closely.

"Do you have a name?" I asked, thinking that

maybe telling each other our names would get this relationship into a more…personal direction.

"Arys."

"Okay." I smiled, feeling a tiny bit more comfortable now. "My name is Penelope."

He looked at me like I had just told him the strangest name imaginable. "Too long."

I frowned. "What do you mean, *too long*?"

"I call you human."

"What? No, my name is Penelope. You have to call me that if you want to be my friend."

"Friend?" He looked amused. "I am not your friend. I am your mate."

A cramp hit me, and I crossed my arms over my stomach. My frown deepened. "Okay, but I don't want to be called *human*."

"Penelope is too long."

"Call me Pen, then," I suggested. "It's my nickname."

"Nickname?"

"Yes, a shorter version of someone's name. Don't you have nicknames around here?"

"No, we have one name. Short. Normal."

I had never heard of the name *Arys* before. It was beautiful, though. It suited him.

"Okay. That's fair." I continued to study him and decided to move on from this conversation. "How do *you* feel?"

"Good," he said, nonchalant. "I go hunt now."

"Alone?"

"Yes. You can not hunt."

I was starting to take all these insults to heart. But he was right. I couldn't hunt. "Okay. And what do I do?"

"You stay here. Wait. Sit. Or you leave."

"Leave?" I was starting to sound just like him. Using single words to communicate.

"Yes."

"Why would I leave?"

"Because I am giving you a choice. If you leave, I will not look for you again. If you stay, it means you give fate a chance," he stated, and with one more intense look, he turned around and left through a big opening.

I stood there, following him with my eyes until he disappeared in the distance. He left me in his cave, and it was for me to decide if I wanted to stay or leave.

It was a bit unfair to be honest, seeing as I had no idea how I'd get back home from here.

I bit the inside of my cheeks and turned my head to look around, taking in my surroundings. This cave wasn't really a cave. There was a large opening at the top, and two more on the sides, allowing me to see far across the Land of Everything. I could see the forest and a lake from here, and when I turned around, there was another opening leading further into the mountain.

I guess that's where we came from, as he told me that he wanted to get me to the other side of the mountain last night.

He had left me a choice, and I wasn't sure what to

do. There was a reason why I wanted to come here. He was the reason, and now that I found him, did I really want to leave again?

Or did I want to find out what this between us could become?

The most logical thing to do was to leave. It would've been the right decision if this intense pull didn't keep me here.

I took a step toward one of the openings, and as I longed for him to come back, I knew I had to stay.

I need to give him a try.

***

There was a spring running along one side of the cave, and since I felt dirty and desperately needed to clean myself after all the walking I had done yesterday, I decided to wash myself in there.

The water had just the right temperature, and after undressing to my underwear, I sat right into the stream and washed my body with the clear spring water.

I washed my clothes as well, and I laid them out into the sun to dry.

After a while, I got back up and sat out by one of the entrances to dry off. There were no towels around, and I wondered if he even had anything remotely close to human things.

Though, seeing as he had fur, he probably just dried off like an animal.

There were many things I'd have to ask him, but the most intriguing thing to find out was how he lived in this cave without the most normal utilities.

I planned on asking him many questions once he would be back, and seeing as I had already made my decision to stay, I got comfortable on the little patch of grass right outside the cave and waited for him to come back.

CHAPTER 4

PENELOPE

I had no way to track time, but after what seemed like forever, Arys was coming back. I couldn't see him yet, but my stomach started to cramp again, and that was a definite sign that he was getting close again.

I wasn't sure why the pain hadn't come back while he was gone. Maybe it was a sign that I had made the right decision. Either way, I was glad he was coming back because I was hungry.

I had gotten dressed a while ago, and once he appeared on the trail leading up to the cave, I stood up and smiled at him.

"Hi," I said.

He stopped and looked at me as if he was trying to decide if I was really there. He was holding something over his shoulder, and when he lifted his arm, I saw a bunch of rabbits hanging from a rope in his hand.

My face fell. That was supposed to be my food?

"You made your decision," he stated, putting the rabbits down, along with a bunch of bushes that had berries on them.

I slowly nodded and pressed my lips into a thin line.

"Though, I'm not so sure I understand what my decision means," I told him truthfully.

He grunted and waved his large hand at me. "It means you are mine now. You stayed."

Fair enough.

I kept on studying the rabbits and wondered if I could at least cook them first. "Can we make a fire?"

He looked at me as if I had just asked him to do the impossible. "I don't make fire."

"Don't you eat?"

He kept looking at me like I was the strangest creature here, when it was clearly him who was weird. "No. I am not weak."

"But everyone needs to eat. If I make a fire to roast the rabbits, will you eat with me?" I asked, smiling up at him again.

He was huge, and I had to put my head into my neck to see his face.

"I do not eat," he told me, sounding annoyed with me trying to get him to eat.

I would get him to join me. Right now, I had to make a fire and eat because I was starving.

Arys kept watching me as I ate another piece of meat, nibbling at the bone to get as much off it as I could. Rabbits didn't have too much meat on them, but one was enough for me. I kept picking berries off the thin branches. They were sweet but occasionally had a sour taste to them.

"Are you sure you don't want any? I can't eat them all," I told him.

He was sitting on the other side of the fire, with his hands in his lap.

"I do not eat," he repeated.

"But why? Don't you need food too?"

"No. I just need shadows."

I frowned. "And how does one eat shadows?"

"I consume them."

"Consume them how?" I asked, surprised.

He stared down at me, with his eyes glowing brighter than before. He was trying to figure out how to explain to me his way of eating.

"I thrive from shadows the same way plants thrive from sunlight."

I needed a moment to understand what he meant, and though I wasn't fully convinced that I comprehended it, I nodded. "I see. Have you been consuming my shadow since I've been here?"

"Yes."

I pursed my lips. "Is that why people call you a shadow creature?"

He nodded, then he pointed at the rabbits next to me. "Eat more."

"I can't eat them all. You should try one. Maybe you can feed on other things too, and not just shadows. It's delicious," I promised him as I held one of the rabbits up.

He studied it, and after a while, he finally grabbed it with his forefinger and thumb. He lifted it up to his face, observing it closely before opening his mouth and dropping the animal onto his tongue.

I watched him chew it, hearing the bones crack in his mouth as he bit down on them.

"Do you like it?"

"Not my favorite."

"So you rather feed on tasteless shadows than actual meat?" I asked, amused by his expression.

"Yes."

I laughed and finished the piece of meat I had in my hands, and after throwing aside the bone, I got up to wash my hands in the spring.

"By the way...do you have towels or blankets?" Asking that question made me realize that I had brought two warm blankets, but ever since waking up here this morning, the backpack was gone. "My backpack..."

"You do not need blankets. I will keep you warm."

I furrowed my brows and turned to look at him. "I left my backpack on the other side of the mountain. I need to go get it."

"You do not need blankets!" he growled, raising his deep voice.

I wanted to argue with him, but the way he was looking at me told me that it wouldn't work anyway.

I took a deep breath to keep calm, and with my arms crossed over my chest, I took in his full size as he stood in front of me. "When I wash myself, I need to dry off. I can't do that without a towel. I need one. Humans need things you don't need."

He watched me, and it looked like he was trying to figure out what I was saying. "What kind of towel?" he then asked.

"Just a simple towel. A piece of fabric. Like... like that." I pointed at the large piece of fabric he had around his hips. It covered the majority of his crotch, but longer fur came out the sides. A piece of it covered his backside too, and the base of his long tail was holding it up.

Arys looked down at himself, pinching the brown fabric between his claws.

"Where did you get that?" I asked, hoping he could get me one as well. Or more than one, so I could have blankets and towels.

He shrugged. "Outside."

Right. That wasn't very helpful.

"Do you think I can get one of those too? Just a smaller size?"

He thought about it for a while before his eyes met mine again. "Okay. Tomorrow."

"Thank you, Arys." I smiled up at him, and while he kept standing there, I moved closer to him, taking in the fabric covering what I imagined was his private part.

Why else would he be wearing that?

Curiosity took over me, and I admired his body from head to toe, before my eyes got a glimpse of that long tail swinging behind him.

I had noticed it before, but I didn't give it much attention.

His tail was long and thick, with the tip looking like a rounded arrowhead. It twitched every once in a while, and it looked as if it moved along with his slow and steady breathing.

Once I moved my eyes to his front side, I admired his large chest. His pecs looked hard, but after sleeping on it for a night, I could say confidently that it wasn't as hard as it looked. The fur covering his skin made his body soft.

Lowering my gaze, I took in his stomach. It looked like it was carved out of stone. Either that, or Arys worked out a lot to make his muscles show that much.

Though...did creatures in this world work out?

Probably not. They were naturally like this.

Further down his upper body, I took in that fabric covering his crotch again. The fur that ran down along his inner thighs was longer than the fur on the rest of his body.

I studied the brown fabric, wondering what it was covering.

"Do you want to see it?" he asked, his voice low.

I furrowed my brows and looked up at him. "*It?*"

"My tool for mating and breeding," he told me.

He calls his cock a tool?

I frowned harder. "I'm not sure. It looks big."

Arys chuckled, his glowing eyes amused. "Of course it is big. I am big too."

"Yeah, we have established that," I murmured.

Without asking again or waiting for a response, he pulled aside the fabric to reveal his *tool*.

I gasped, shocked by the size of his shaft.

That's when I started to understand what was supposed to happen with us.

The pain I had came from the need to mate, and it so happened that Arys was the one who had the power to make this pain go away.

The only thing was…his tool was as large as my leg, and there was no way that thing would take away the pain.

It would only make it worse, I worried.

CHAPTER 5

PENELOPE

I couldn't stop staring at it.

I was mesmerized by its size, and by the dark shades of purple it had.

The tip of it looked soft, and there was no hair on it. Well, not that I was expecting any of it.

God, I had no expectations of what it looked like, to be honest.

Seeing as Arys was a shadow creature, everything about him was surprising.

The sketch I had of him didn't have a cock on it. Only a tail, and though it didn't quite look the same, it had a slight resemblance to the one in the drawing.

"You can touch it," he encouraged as he reached between his legs to squeeze it.

I looked up at him, and his expression was soft. He must've noticed how nervous I was, but he could also sense my curiosity.

"I don't think I'm ready to touch it," I admitted, dropping my gaze to his length again.

I watched as he rubbed it with his fist, and every time he reached the tip, he squeezed it gently, rubbing his thumb over it.

He was doing it sensually, and just by watching him please himself, I felt waves of excitement flood through my body.

Maybe I did want to touch it. Maybe…it's what I needed to do.

Swallowing the saliva that had formed in my mouth, I took a step forward and reached out my hand. He stopped rubbing himself and tightened his grip at the base of his cock as he watched me closely.

I placed my hand on the side of his shaft, and as my skin touched his, his cock twitched. It was warm and soft, but it hardened under my touch.

Looking up at him, I saw his face slowly tense. He looked pleased, but his eyes darkened at my touch.

"You are a delicate human. I like that," he told me in his deep voice.

Biting back a smile, I looked back at his cock and admired the tip.

I wasn't sure if I could touch it, but I slowly moved my fingers along the side until I was close enough to it. Looking up into his eyes again, I noticed that they had turned black. Maybe that was normal for when he was being touched.

But I didn't question it.

"Can I touch you here?" I asked, nodding my head toward his tip.

"Yes."

I could tell he was a bit reluctant for me to do so, and knowing human penises were sensitive at the tip too, I figured being gentle was the best option.

My fingers grazed the rounded tip and sensitive flesh, and it twitched as I got closer to the small hole at the very top. Without giving me a warning, a drop of white liquid formed, and Arys shifted on his feet, almost as if he was struggling to control himself.

I kept looking up into his face to make sure what I was doing wasn't overwhelming him. Then again… I couldn't believe that the touch of my small hands was too much for him.

"Is this okay?" I asked, reaching up with my other hand to place it on the other side of his length.

"Yes." His short reply told me just how much he enjoyed my touch, even if it made him tense.

While I continued to touch his cock, and drops of what I assumed was his cum rolled down his tip, I noticed his tail curl around my left leg.

When I looked down, I noticed the tip of it glistening in the sunlight. It looked wet, and whenever it touched my skin, it left a trace. As I inspected it further, I noticed a small slit across the tip, with light purple liquid coming out of it.

"I can not always control it," he told me through gritted teeth. "It is looking for a fertile woman."

I looked up at him again, surprised by his words. "Can it be used for breeding too?" I asked, my voice almost a whisper.

Arys nodded as his tail moved further up my leg, wrapping around it like a rope. When I dropped my gaze to his cock, I noticed that it was fully erect now. It had gotten bigger, and I took a step back, stumbling as his tail kept me from moving my leg.

His large hand cupped me from behind, and I leaned against the palm of it, pressing not only my back but also my hands against him. My mind was starting to get foggy, and I needed to press my legs together to ease the tension I was feeling.

"What are you feeling?" he asked, and I lifted my gaze again to look into his eyes.

"Lust." It hadn't been on my mind, but it was what my body was feeling. "I can't move."

"That means you want this to happen," he stated.

"With your tail?"

"Yes. It needs you too. I can make it stop but it can ease the pain inside of you."

I watched him closely as he spoke, and his tail kept tickling the inside of my thighs, trying to part my legs.

Its wetness tickled my skin, and every single touch felt like an electric shock that moved through my veins.

As intense as he made me feel, I figured that Arys must've been feeling the same. It was him who needed to mate with me, and his tail was simply doing the work to get us there.

"We can stop," he told me, but I quickly shook my head.

"No, I need it," I whispered.

I reached down to unbutton my shorts, and after sliding them down my legs, followed by my underwear, I stepped out of it with my right leg.

His tail retracted as I had covered parts of it with my clothing, and after it pulled away from the shorts, it moved back up my leg, curling around it like before.

His tip slid further up my inner thigh, and I widened my stance so it had better access to my pussy. I couldn't take my eyes off it as it got closer to my entrance, and once he pressed against it, I threw my head back with a gasp.

"Oh!"

"Relax," Arys told me, and I opened my eyes to look up at him again.

"Will it be gentle?" I asked, hoping that there wouldn't be even more pain I had to deal with.

"It will feel good," he assured me. "For you and me."

I pressed my lips together tightly and looked down to watch as the tip of his tail slid through my folds. It rubbed against my clit a few times, making my legs shake.

His liquid kept coming out of it, and he spread it all over my folds, wetting my entrance as well.

Moaning, I threw my head back and closed my eyes to help myself relax. It felt like the liquid was intoxicating my body, and I wondered if it made Arys feel the same. He hadn't stopped pumping his large cock with his hand though, so I figured he was enjoying this as well.

After a while of teasing me, the tip pressed against my entrance, and I opened my eyes again to watch it. It moved back and forth, trying to enter me. The tip was thick and about the size of a man's fist, but it felt soft.

"Oh..." I moaned, parting my legs even more to give it enough room.

When it finally pushed into me, I held my breath and gripped one of Arys' fingers behind me. He was holding me in place, and I needed him to steady me before my knees gave in.

I felt the tip of his tail push into me more, and once it was inside, it slid inside as deep as it could before stopping. It was letting me adjust to its size, and once I finally was able to breathe again, I felt my body relax more.

It was stretching me, and filling me with that liquid that had been oozing out of it before.

"How does it feel?" Arys asked. His voice sounded amused, and when I looked up at him, there was a pleased gleam in his eyes.

"It feels good," I told him with a soft cry as his tail pulled out of me before slamming back into me.

Every good emotion imaginable hit me out of nowhere, and I threw my head back again with my eyes closed, and my grip tightening on his finger. "Holy shit!"

His tail started to penetrate me, and I let it, starting to enjoy this. I've had sex before, but nothing was comparable to this.

The thickness of the tail was stretching me from the inside, and while it didn't hurt, it did feel uncomfortable at first until I got used to its size. The pleasure I felt quickly took over, and the longer he kept fucking me, the more I could enjoy it.

I hadn't looked down to see what he was doing

to me yet, but it felt as if every time he pushed back into me, I took in more of his tail. My belly felt full and bloated, but it wasn't hurting.

When I finally urged myself to look down, I saw a bump on my lower stomach, indicating where the tip ended. I dared to place my hand on it, and though it felt strange, I started to smile.

How could something so unusual make me feel this desperate for more?

My touch made the tail twitch inside of me, and when I looked up, I noticed that my touch affected Arys too. "Do you feel this?" I asked, rubbing my hand over my bump again.

"Yes," he hissed through gritted teeth.

"Do you like it when I do this?"

He nodded, continuing to rub his shaft with his other hand. I could see his body starting to crouch over me, and it looked as if he wasn't able to stand there like that any longer.

It turned out that I was right because he picked me up gently, and walked over to the patch of grass outside the cave. He placed me on the grass, and I kept looking up at him as he knelt before me, still rubbing his cock.

His tail hadn't left me, and it kept fucking me in a steady rhythm. It went in and out, pushing deeper with every thrust.

I moaned as an intense wave came over me, and it felt like I was about to orgasm. I hadn't had one of those in a while, and to be honest, I hadn't expected for the next thing to make me come to be a shadow creature's tail.

His groans got louder too, and just hearing him grunt while he watched me getting fucked by his tail turned me on a lot.

The first orgasm hit me out of nowhere, and I cried out as it washed through me. My body shook and my hips lifted off the ground, but with the tail still inside of me, it pushed me back down, holding me in place. My legs were shaking, and I clung to the grass so hard that it kept ripping out of the ground.

The tail started to throb against my walls, and just as I was about to come back down from my high, his liquid filled me, leaving me in a state of shock as a second orgasm rolled on.

I couldn't think straight, but once I calmed down again, I had no doubt about the fact that whatever that liquid was, it had a special, pleasurable effect on me.

"Fuuuck!" I moaned loudly, trying to wiggle away from it. I wanted it to pull out of my body, but it kept me right in place. It seemed as if I couldn't stop coming.

I looked up at Arys and whimpered, watching as his expression changed. He was still stroking himself and tensed shortly after squeezing his tip. A deep growl tore from his chest, and a long string of cum hit my body. It coated my skin, and as surprised as I was, I kept my eyes on his face as he continued to shoot his load onto my body.

During all of this, his tail continued to thrust into me and fill me with its juices. My body felt heavy, and my head light.

Arys struck his cock one last time before he fell to his side next to me on the grass. His tail stayed inside of me, but because I was so full, the liquid oozed out of me.

"How much longer–" I breathed deeply and looked down, seeing my stomach all round and bloated. "When will it stop?"

"It will not move out until it softens," Arys told me, sounding just as out of breath as I was.

"What...how?"

"It is like a knot."

I furrowed my brows and tried to understand what he meant. "Like...an animal's penis?"

He nodded, though he didn't seem to like the way I put it. "It stays inside of you until it softens," he repeated, sounding determined.

"And..." I took another deep breath. "Will it stop releasing that liquid inside of me?"

It was making me feel incredible things, but I wasn't sure I could keep handling it.

"Eventually."

"You don't know exactly?" I stared down to where his tail disappeared inside of me.

"No."

I lifted my gaze again, and after a moment of studying his face, I realized that Arys probably never had sex before. Or, his tail never had.

"Was this your first time?" I asked, smiling gently.

He nodded, his brows furrowed deeply. "You are my fated mate."

He said those words as if he was stating the fact that he couldn't sleep with anyone else because I was the one who was meant for him.

In a way, it was quite romantic.

On the other hand...I still needed to get along with the idea of having a fated mate.

One that was a sixteen-feet-tall shadow creature who lived in the Land of Everything.

CHAPTER 6

PENELOPE

I woke up in the middle of the night as something moved inside of me. When I opened my eyes to look down, I noticed that I was lying on top of Arys, just like I had the other night.

He must've picked me up after I fell asleep earlier, and he didn't seem to mind all of his cum that was covering my body. It had since dried on my skin, and I felt a little icky.

His tail was moving again, and it pulled out of me slowly, making my stomach flat again.

I turned onto my back and covered my belly with both hands, still feeling full, even without him there anymore.

"Are you okay, Pen?" His low growl interrupted the silence, and I turned my head to look up at him.

"Yes. I think so," I whispered. "I feel dirty."

His hand came up, and he gently covered me with it. "I will clean you in the morning. You need to rest now."

I nodded, not fighting him on that.

I was sleepy, and after everything that happened last night, I also needed to clear my mind.

I kept looking into his eyes, smiling gently as the warmth of his golden gaze soothed me. I could tell that he was worried about me.

"I will have to get used to this. I'm just a bit overwhelmed," I told him.

He studied me closely, needing a moment to understand why I said that. "You are meant for me like I am meant for you. You have to get used to this," he demanded.

I laughed softly and gave him another nod. I patted his fingers and curled up underneath his hand. "I will. Don't worry, Arys."

***

The sun was shining bright in my face, and when I opened my eyes, I was met with the most beautiful view over the Land of Everything. The sky was blue and the trees looked healthy, and on the far right, the lake shimmered in an almost transparent glow.

I was on the grass again, but I had something covering my body. When I looked at it, I noticed that it was the fabric that Arys used to wear around his hips to cover his cock.

I didn't want to get up yet, but his presence was missing, and I wanted to find him. Once I pushed myself up, I looked into the cave to find him standing with his back to me. He was where I had created the bonfire last night, and it looked like he had made another fire.

I slowly got up, with my legs still shaking, but I managed to stand up straight.

Arys turned around as I walked toward him with the fabric wrapped around my body, and he quickly studied me to make sure I was okay.

"Are you in pain, Pen?" he asked.

I smiled at him and shook my head. "No, I feel okay. Just a little...weak."

"You have to eat, then wash," he told me, pointing back at the fire behind him. "I got you food."

When I looked around his legs, I noticed a large animal hanging over the fire. It looked like a deer. Though, it didn't matter what it was. I was hungry, and I just wanted to eat.

"Thank you. Will you eat with me?" I asked, looking up at him again.

"No. I am full."

I narrowed my eyes and decided not to ask any further questions. He didn't look too pleased with the state I was in, and to keep him happy, I accepted his choice not to eat with me.

My eyes dropped to his cock because it was just... there. Uncovered. Large. Magnificent.

I pressed my lips into a thin line and hugged my body tighter with the fabric he usually covered his cock with. "Do you want this back?" I asked.

"No. You keep it. It is yours now."

"Thank you."

I still couldn't take my eyes off his cock.

It was hanging there between his legs in all of its glory, and a couple of intriguing ideas crossed my mind. Ones that before last night I wouldn't have dared to think about.

"What?" he asked, looking down at me with a raised brow.

"Nothing. I was just thinking…"

"About what?"

I thought about my question and held my breath before speaking. "Will you ever be able to fuck me with your cock?" My cheeks immediately blushed, even with all the courage I had collected to ask.

His eyes were still on me, and his body had eased after hearing that question. "Hopefully. If you let me."

"I'll let you. I just don't…understand how it will work."

He led me to the fire with one hand, making me sit down by the fire. "It will work."

"Okay…but how?" I asked, amused.

"You are meant for me. Have some faith in the fates, Pen."

I understood that there wouldn't be any other answer that would explain just how the sex with him would work, so I accepted his words and changed the subject.

"Will you take a bath with me after I eat?"

He grunted. "Maybe."

He was a big grump. I pursed my lips in amusement. "Pretty please?"

He groaned as if taking a bath with me was the worst thing in the world. "Maybe," he repeated. "Eat first."

Fine then.

I would find ways to make him less grumpy.

Although, I did like the way he was. He was the exact opposite of me, and I liked how contrasting our characters were.

Maybe it was the right thing to stay and be with him.

Maybe…a life with him would be just what I needed to finally feel complete.

CHAPTER 7

PENELOPE

After successfully convincing Arys to take a bath with me, he wanted to show me around the Land of Everything. His intentions were to make sure that I knew my way back here in case I'd ever get lost.

I wasn't sure why I would ever get lost around here though, let alone wander around by myself. Arys wouldn't take his eyes off me, and he sure as hell wouldn't let me run around without being in his sight at all times.

He had called me weak two times already this morning.

Well, he didn't say it directly to my face.

He said I wouldn't be strong enough to find my way back to him because the Land of Everything was a confusing place. I argued with him that if I'd ever get lost, the pull between us would take me back to him, but he said that wouldn't work anymore since we already had sex.

Well, I had sex with his tail.

God, it was still confusing.

We walked through the dark cave system inside the mountain and ended up coming out on the other side where he first found me. From there, we headed down to the forest, and I walked beside him as we passed tall trees and bushes with colorful flowers and berries.

There were bird sounds coming from all around us, and though this place was huge, it seemed like we were the only ones around here. It was so quiet, and even his heavy footsteps were silenced by the moss covering the ground.

"Why do humans call it the Land of Everything?" he asked, breaking the silence. He was looking down at me as we continued to walk through the forest.

I smiled. "Because although we don't know much about it, we believe that there is nothing we can't imagine that lives here."

"Stupid."

I frowned. "What's stupid?"

"The name."

Fair enough.

"I'm not going to argue with that," I said with a chuckle and looked around as he stopped. "What is this place?"

It looked like the trees around us formed a circle, and multiple paths led into different directions.

"This is the middle of the Dark Forest. It is not a good place for humans to be," he explained, looking down at me. "Usually."

"But I am safe with you, right?"

"Yes." He grunted as if he wasn't pleased with himself.

"But you didn't necessarily want to bring me

here."

"No."

I pursed my lips and looked around. "I haven't seen any other creatures yet."

"They are watching us."

"What?"

"They are watching us," he repeated, his jaw tight as he spoke. "But they won't attack you because you are with me."

That was good to know. It was still unsettling.

He noticed me tensing up, and he pulled me closer to him with his hand cupping my back. "Do not worry, Pen. You are safe with me. But..."

"But?"

"When there is a weak female, we put them on a leash."

First of all...he indirectly called me weak for the third time.

Secondly...a leash?

"I don't understand."

He turned to look at me while keeping his hand behind me. He was protecting me from whatever was hiding in the bushes.

"The females that live around here are smaller. Not as small and weak as you are..."

Four times.

"But we still protect them."

"By putting them on a leash? What kind of leash?"

"The tail. It enters the female and stays there," he explained, making it sound like it was the most normal thing.

I studied him and decided that the idea of that didn't sit right with me. "I don't think I want that."

A gentle expression softened his face, accepting my decision. "You do not have to, Pen. But our females benefit from it. It pleasures them too."

I nodded but didn't want to continue this conversation, and so I let him lead me further into the forest.

He talked about all the places in the Land of Everything. Well, he still didn't call it that. To him, this place was just home.

He explained to me that in the north, there was the Great Valley, in the east, the Neverending Desert, and in the west, there were the Thousand Lakes. I wondered about other creatures, since in all the books I read there were hundreds, if not thousands.

Arys started to list creatures I had never heard of before, proving to me that what us humans knew about this place was just a smidge. The creatures he told me about that stuck with me were the ones living in the waters. Some sort of mixture between mermaids and kraken. The wolves that were as big as bears also intrigued me, but I would never want to stumble across one of them.

The sun was slowly setting, and he told me that we had to get back to the cave. On our way back, I couldn't shake the idea of scary creatures hiding around us, watching and following us. The noises sounding in the distance didn't help me keep my mind at ease.

Although I was sure that no one would dare to step forward with Arys walking right next to me, I couldn't shake the idea of what would happen if a creature was stupid enough to attack us. I didn't want to get hurt, and I didn't want to be mistaken as an intruder either.

I kept looking around, and every time I did, his tail came up behind me in a protective masser. It pulled me closer to Arys' side, and it seemed as if the tail was doing all that on its own–out of pure instinct.

I knew Arys wasn't indifferent about this though. When I looked up at him, I saw the distress in his face. He didn't like walking beside me without his tail inside of me. As my mate, he was supposed to keep me on a leash, to show everyone else in this land that I belonged to him, and that I wasn't here to harm anyone.

I swallowed and stopped while reaching out to grab one of his fingers. "Arys?" I said, keeping my voice low. "I want to try it."

"Try what?"

"Your tail. I want it inside of me. You know this world better than I do, and I...trust you," I told him with a gentle smile. "So, if you think it is safer for me to be on a leash, then so be it."

His full body eased, and all the tension in his face disappeared. He looked satisfied with my words, and I already felt more secure.

"As you wish, Pen. You will enjoy it," he declared with a pleased smile.

I pursed my lips.

I did enjoy what his tail had done to me last night, but it was the liquid that came out of it that made me feel a certain way.

I looked down as his tail trailed up my leg, and since the shorts I was wearing were loose enough, it easily moved under it. His liquid spread on my skin, and it affected me a lot already, without him penetrating me just yet.

I didn't have time to question why that liquid was so intoxicated once it touched my skin, as his tip pushed past my underwear, and inserted itself into my pussy.

I moaned and looked up at him as I steadied myself against his hand.

He was watching me closely as his tail twisted inside of me, pushing as deep into me as it could. "How does it feel?" he asked.

"Good."

"Do you think you can walk?"

I nodded, but I needed to stand still for a moment as his tail pulled out of me slightly, just to push inside again. "Oh God…" I moaned quietly.

I raised a brow at him, watching as his pleased smile turned into a grin. "Told you."

"Yeah, you did tell me. But you didn't mention that it will fuck me all the way back to the cave."

I couldn't walk and orgasm at the same time, but Arys had the brightest idea on how to avoid it.

"Just hold back," he suggested.

Right. As if it's that easy.

I sighed and focused on my body, and once I was ready to walk, we continued along the mossy path to get back to the cave before the darkness rolled in.

CHAPTER 8

PENELOPE

The whole way back, I couldn't think about anything other than his tail pushing me closer to an orgasm.

I had tried my hardest not to come, but the tension inside of me was getting unbearable. So much so that I desperately needed him.

It was torture feeling his tail and those juices inside of me, and I needed release.

I let myself fall onto the grass right by the cave entrance, and after turning onto my back, I closed my eyes and sighed heavily.

"Are you all right?" Arys asked, his voice filled with worry. I felt him sit down next to me, and his hand covered my stomach gently.

"Yes, just a little tired and..." I stopped myself, unsure if he would understand the word I held back.

"And? Tell me," he demanded.

I opened my eyes and looked up at him. I had to tell him if I wanted this tension to go away. "Horny. I'm horny and I think I need you, Arys."

He raised a brow at me before his eyes wandered between my legs where his tail was still slowly fucking me.

It hadn't stopped, and I was slowly going crazy.

"I am already doing it."

"I don't mean with your tail." I dropped my gaze to his crotch where his semi-hard cock was to indicate what I meant.

"Are you sure?"

I frowned. "I think so."

"That is not enough. You need to be sure."

A moan left my lips, and I parted my legs to let his tail fuck me deeper. "Yes. Yes, I'm sure!"

He kept on studying me. *He* was the unsure one.

"Do you think it won't work?"

"It will take a while. I do not wish to hurt you. I will need time," he explained as he caressed my belly with his fingers. He still looked indecisive. "Are you sure?" he asked again.

"Yes." My reply was way more determined now. "I think we are meant to do it. You said it yourself, Arys. I was made for you, so it has to work somehow."

As if those words were what he needed to hear, he got back up and knelt in front of me. He took in the sight before him, and while he did, his tail stretched me from within.

It was a strange feeling, but it didn't hurt. That liquid that continuously came out of him not only felt good, but it eased any possible pain.

Maybe that was the reason why I was able to take him in.

Almost like...magic.

His eyes were turning black again, with lust

washing over his face to show me just how much he wanted this too.

I moaned and rested my head on the grass while keeping my eyes on his. The liquid kept on filling me, but it dripped out of me, rolling down the inside of my thighs.

I was so wet that his tail moved in and out of me with ease, and I had a feeling that even his big cock would be able to do that without a problem.

"I think you are ready for me, Pen," he murmured as he rubbed his shaft with one hand. I watched it grow under his touch, and I smiled at him, wanting him to know that I was excited for this.

But as prepared as I was, I wasn't ready for what he said next.

"I will pick you up now."

"Pick me up?"

"Yes. It will be easier that way," he told me.

I had no idea what he meant by that, but once he picked me up with one hand, I started to understand what his intentions were.

He held me in the palm of his hand, with his thumb holding up my head. My legs were spread wide open as he positioned me in front of him. That's when I started to get nervous about his size.

"Slow, okay?" I said, swallowing hard.

"You do not have to worry, my Penelope. I will be gentle."

Those words sounded comical coming out of his mouth, seeing as he was a giant with huge body parts, and I was just a tiny woman compared to him.

The need to have him inside of me increased with every second, and my pussy clenched every time I dropped my gaze to his cock.

I needed release, and Arys seemed to have caught on to it.

His tail suddenly released a large amount of liquid inside of me, and I cried out as the first orgasm washed over me.

"Oh, God!"

If it was that easy for him to make me come with just his tail, I was worried that just by the touch of his cock, my body would explode.

His tail pulled out of me then, and the juices oozed out of me. It felt like he had left a hole inside of my body, and though I wasn't in pain, I was pretty sure my organs had shifted to make space for his cock.

I watched intently as he moved his tip closer to my pussy, and as it touched my entrance, an intense shiver rushed through my body.

"Arys…" I whispered, trying to reach out my hands to stop him from moving any closer.

"Shhh, it will be okay," he assured, smiling gently. "I will be careful with you, my Penelope."

I swallowed the lump that had formed at the back of my throat, then I held my breath when his tip pushed against my opening.

He moved slowly, pushing me down on his cock. It took him a while to get the tip inside, and I already felt full.

"Oh!" I cried out and threw my head back with my

eyes closed. "How...how is that possible?"

He didn't have an answer for that. To be fair, he couldn't have known that his fated mate was me–a human.

"Does it feel good?" he asked instead.

"Yes. I think so. I mean...it doesn't hurt," I told him in a shaky voice. "I'm just confused."

He muttered something under his breath before his hips moved forward. His face tensed, and I figured it was his own juices that made him feel the same intense feeling that I experienced.

"Tight," he grunted, but that didn't seem to bother him. "I will go deeper."

"Okay. Just...just go slow, please."

His eyes met mine as the tension in his face eased. "I will not hurt you. I will never hurt my human," he stated with determination.

He continued to move his tip in and out of me, and with every push forward, I took in more of his length. When I looked down, there was a bump on my stomach. Smiling, I gently moved my hand over it. Arys was watching me, and the way I caressed the bump encouraged him to push me down on his cock even more. After a while, his cock completely disappeared inside of me.

I had never felt this fulfilled.

Pun intended.

"You are doing so well," he praised.

I smiled up at him as I felt my body relax.

"You can move now," I told him.

He eyed me for a moment before starting to move

again, and every time he pushed forward, my belly rose.

It was an indescribable feeling, but I wanted more of it. I wanted to feel that way forever.

"Fuck, yes." I moaned and closed my eyes again as he started to thrust in and out of me in a slow and steady rhythm.

His groans got louder, and just hearing him getting pleasure because of me turned me on even more. We were both about to reach a high that should've been impossible to reach, but the harder he fucked me, the closer we got to it.

My clit ached, needing some attention, and I reached down to rub it with my fingers. He started to pulsate inside of me, and as his hips stopped moving, he moved me instead.

He was using me like a pump, and it didn't take long for him to reach his climax.

"Gah! You are so tight around my cock. You are made for me. You are perfect for me." He kept complimenting and praising me, and his words pushed me right over the edge.

His cum filled me as my body shook uncontrollably. His groans were loud, and I was certain that they could be heard in all of the Land of Everything.

"Take my seed, Pen," he encouraged, pumping more of his warm liquid inside of me. "You are my mate. You belong to me."

"Yes! OH GOD YES!"

It took a while to calm back down from the high

he made me reach, and even with his cock softening inside me, the pleasure still rolled over me.

My legs were shaking as he pulled out of me, and after he laid down on his back, he gently placed me on top of him.

I was exhausted.

Closing my eyes, I tried my best to breathe calmly.

We were both silent, but I let out a surprised squeal when I felt his tail teasing at my entrance. "What is it doing?" I asked, just as it entered me again.

I wasn't ready for round two. I needed rest before we did that all over again. But it wasn't doing what I thought it was.

"It wants to keep the remaining cum inside of you," Arys murmured, sounding half asleep already. "It's where it belongs."

CHAPTER 9

PENELOPE

Exhausted wasn't the right word to describe the way I was feeling.

I was tired, and though all I wanted to do was sleep, I felt happy and content with how life was at the moment. I didn't want to miss a thing, but I couldn't stay awake day after day.

A few days had passed, and spending them with Arys taught me new things about this land, and about myself. I was even getting used to having his tail inside of me. It was as if Arys couldn't get enough of me, but I wouldn't complain.

My feelings for him had intensified, and the way I saw it, it wasn't possible to move on from here.

I was meant to be with him.

I *wanted* to be with him, and while it seemed impossible, I wanted to spend forever with him.

Arys had brought me another deer tonight for dinner, and afterward, we sat outside the cave, watching the sun go down over the Land of Everything.

I leaned against his leg, with my head resting on his soft fur, and his hand gently caressing my back.

I took in the colors of the sky, admiring the soft purple and orangey color.

I was fascinated by the beauty of this place, and I wondered if anything had ever destroyed it.

"Arys?"

"Hm?"

"Has this place ever been destroyed by something? Like…a wildfire or a landslide," I asked, looking away from the colorful sky and up at the most handsome creature I had ever seen.

My creature.

"No. Nothing can ever destroy this land," he told me.

I pursed my lips and studied his face before looking straight ahead again. "Nothing? Not even the creatures living in it?"

"No. We would never destroy our home. It is stupid and disrespectful."

He was right about that.

If only the people in my world would be this careful and kind to the life we were given.

"And what about intruders?"

"If they come here with bad intentions, we make sure they leave again. We do not want intruders here." He turned his head and nudged me closer against his body. "Why do you ask such horrible questions, Pen?"

I didn't think my questions were horrible. I simply wanted to know how it was possible for them to live here in such peace and quiet, when in the real world, there were ongoing, unnecessary wars.

I shrugged. "Maybe because I still can't believe that this world exists."

"It does. You are in it."

I laughed softly at his grumpy statement. "I'm aware of that. It's still pretty unbelievable. I mean, I won't be able to tell anyone about my time here. They would think I'm crazy."

Arys grunted. "You are not crazy. You think poorly of yourself."

Smirking, I turned more toward him and said in a mocking tone, "Well, it was you who kept on calling me a weak human."

"But I am not anymore. You are not weak. You proved it." He looked at me with a frown. "You are my strong female."

As comical as some of our conversations were, I knew how truthful and honest our words always were.

In just a short amount of time, Arys had shown me just how much he wanted me to stay. We hadn't spoken about it yet, and I figured it was finally time.

"Arys, can I ask you a serious question?" I reached up to take his hand, holding it in front of me, and caressing each of his large fingers.

"I do not like serious."

"No?" I chuckled. "That's funny, because you're quite the serious type."

While I found it funny, he proved to me once again that joking about his mood wasn't something he enjoyed. I kissed the palm of his hand and smiled up at him again before continuing. "What happens now? With us?"

He was quiet, thinking about an answer. "You stay here with me. You do not need to go home."

I puckered my lips, thinking about that possibility. But it wasn't one. "I can't just stay here without visiting my home at least once a month, Arys. Besides…I'm a human. I have different needs than you do."

"Like what?" he grunted, not looking pleased.

"Well, like clothes and medicine. I don't mind taking them here if you don't mind," I suggested. It would be difficult to do that, seeing as Arys couldn't come to the real world.

He was silent again, and I knew it was hard for him to comprehend that my life had been much more different than his life was here.

He looked down at me, studying me closely as he decided on what to say next. "You will not leave me."

"Of course not, Arys."

"When you go home, you will come back," he added, sounding determined.

I smiled. He didn't like the idea of being left alone.

I squeezed his fingers and moved as close to him as I possibly could. "I promise you, I will come back. But I need my things to be comfortable in your land. You understand that, don't you?"

He slowly nodded, frowning again. "I do."

"Good. Then…I guess that's it then." A gentle smile tugged at my lips as I looked up at him with admiration. "This is how it will be from now on. You and me. Here."

"In love."

His words surprised me, but it made my heart skip a beat.

Telling him that I loved him hadn't crossed my mind. Not because I didn't feel that way, but because I thought it was a given.

It was nice hearing him say that though.

I pressed another kiss to the palm of his hand and nodded. "In love…"

…And ready to conquer whatever may come our way.

THE END

Printed in Dunstable, United Kingdom